Christmas Outside Of Eden

By
Coningsby Dawson

CHRISTMAS OUTSIDE OF EDEN

I

This is the story the robins tell as they huddle beneath the holly on the Eve of Christmas. They have told it every Christmas Eve since the world started. They commenced telling it long before Christ was born, for their memory goes further back than men's. The Christmas which they celebrate began just outside of Eden, within sight of its gold-locked doors.

The robins have only two stories: one for Christmas and one for Easter. Their Easter story is quite different. It has to do with how they got the splash of red upon their breasts. It was when God's son was hanging on the cross. They wanted to do something to spare him. They were too weak to pull out the nails from his feet and hands; so they tore their little breasts in plucking the thorns one by one from the crown that had been set upon his forehead. Since then God has allowed their breasts to remain red as a remembrance of His gratitude.

But their Christmas story happened long before, when they weren't robin red-breasts but only robins. It is a merry, tender sort of story. They twitter it in a chuckling fashion to their children. If you prefer to hear it first-hand, creep out to the nearest holly-bush on almost any Christmas Eve when snow has made the night all pale and shadowy. If the robins have chosen your holly-bush as their rendezvous and you understand their language, you won't need to read what I have written. Like all true stories, it is much better told than read. It's the story of the first laugh that was ever heard in earth or heaven. To be enjoyed properly it needs the chuckling twitter of the grown-up robins and the squeaky interruptions of the baby birds asking questions. When they get terrifically excited, they jig up and down on the holly-branches and the frozen snow falls with a brittle clatter. Then the mother and father birds say, "Hush!" quite suddenly. No one speaks for a full five seconds. They huddle closer, listening and holding their breath. That's how the story ought to be heard, after night-fall on Christmas Eve, when behind darkened windows little boys and girls have gone to bed early, having hung up their very biggest stockings. Of course I can't tell it that way on paper, but I'll do my best to repeat the precise words in which the robins tell it.

II

It was very long ago at the beginning of all wonders. Sun, moon and stars were new; they wandered about in the clouds uncertainly, calling to one another like ships in a fog. It was the same on earth; neither trees, nor rivers, nor animals were quite sure why they had been created or what was expected of them. They were terribly afraid of doing wrong and they had good reason, for the Man and Woman had done wrong and had been locked out of Eden.

That had happened in April, when the world was three months old. Up to that time everything had gone very well. No one had known what fear was. No one had guessed that anything existed outside the walls of Eden or that there was such a thing as wrong-doing. Animals, trees and rivers had lived together with the Man and the Woman in the high-walled garden as a happy family. If they had wanted to know anything, they had asked the Man; he had always given them answers, even though he had to invent them. They had never dreamt of doubting him—not even the Woman. The reason for this had been God.

Every afternoon God had come stepping down from the sky to walk with the Man through the sun-spangled shadows of the grassy paths. They had heard the kindly rumble of His voice like distant thunder and the little tones of the Man as he asked his questions. At six o'clock regularly God had shaken hands with the Man and climbed leisurely back up the sky-blue stairs that led to Heaven. Because of this the Man had gained a reputation among the animals for being wise. They had thought of him as God's friend. He had given orders to everybody—even to the Woman; and everyone had been proud to obey him.

It had been in April the great change had occurred. There had been all kinds of rumours. The first that had been suspected had been when God had failed to come for His customary walk; the next had been when He had arrived with His face hidden in anger. The trees of Eden had bent and clashed as if a strong wind were blowing. Everything living that was not rooted, had run away to hide. Nevertheless, when God had called to the Man, they had tiptoed nearer to listen. The trouble had seemed to be about some fruit. God had told the Man that he must not pluck it; he had not only plucked it, but had eaten of it. So had the Woman. It had seemed a small matter to make such a fuss about. They had supposed that God's anger would soon blow over and that everything would be again as friendly as before.

And so everything might have been had it not been for the Man. Instead of saying he was sorry, he had started to argue and blame the Woman. At that God had refused to speak with him longer. He had ordered the Man and Woman and all the animals to leave Eden immediately. He had given them no time to pack. Lining them up like soldiers, He had numbered them to make certain that none were missing and then, with the Man and Woman leading, had marched them beyond the walls and locked the golden gates of Eden against them forever.

Since then all had been privation and confusion. The animals, from regarding the Man as their lord, had grown to despise him. They had blamed him for their misfortunes. They had told him that it was his fault that they had lost their happiness and that God walked the earth no more. The woman had told him so most particularly. Of all the created world only the dog and the robin had remained faithful to him. The dog slept across his feet at night to keep them warm and the robin sang to him each dawn that he should not lose courage.

III

Through the world's first summer things had not been so bad, though of course the wilderness that grew outside of Eden was not so comfortable as the garden they had lost. In the garden no one had needed to work: food had grown on the trees to one's hand and, because it was so sheltered, the weather had been always pleasant. It hadn't been necessary to wear clothing; it hadn't been necessary to build houses, for it had never rained. Birds hadn't troubled to make nests, nor rabbits to dig warrens. Everybody had felt perfectly safe to sleep out-of-doors, wherever he happened to find himself, without a thought of protection.

Here in the wilderness it was different. There were no paths. The jungle grew up tall and threatening. Thorns leant out to tear one's flesh. If it hadn't been for the elephant uprooting trees in his fits of temper, no one would have been able to travel anywhere. One by one the animals slunk away and began to lead their own lives independently, making lairs for themselves. Every day that went by they avoided the Man and Woman more and more. At first they used to peep out of the thicket to jeer at their helplessness; soon they learnt to disregard them as if they were not there. From having believed himself to be the wisest of living creatures the Man discovered himself to be the most incompetent. Often and often he would creep to the gold-locked gates and peer between the bars, hoping to see God walking there as formerly. But God walked no more. As He had climbed back into Heaven, He had destroyed the sky-blue stairs behind Him. There was no way in which the Man could reach Him to ask His advice or pardon.

But it was the Woman who caused the Man most unhappiness. It wasn't that she despised and blamed him. He'd grown used to that since leaving Eden. Everybody, except the dog and the robin, despised and blamed him. The Woman caused him unhappiness because she was unwell—really unwell; not just an upset stomach or a headache. In Eden she had always been strong and beautiful, like sunlight leaping on the smooth, green lawn—so white and pink and darting. Her long gold hair had swayed about her like a flame; her white arms had parted it as though she were a swimmer. Her eyes had been shy and merry from dawn to dusk. She had been a darling; never a cross word had she spoken. The furry creatures of the woods had been her playmates and the birds had perched upon her shoulders to sing their finest songs.

Now she was wan and thin as a withered branch. Like the elephant uprooting trees, she often lost her temper. Sometimes she was sorry for her crossness; more often she wasn't. When the Man offered her things to eat, no matter what trouble he'd taken to get them, she'd say she wasn't hungry. And yet he loved her none the less for her perverseness. He was so afraid.... He couldn't have told you of what he was afraid, for nobody had had time to die in the world as yet. He was filled with dread lest, like God, she might vanish and walk the earth no more. So he cudgelled his brains to find things to cure her. He invented wrong remedies, just as in Eden he had invented wrong answers to the animals' questions. He was never certain whether they would do her good or harm; but he always assured her gravely that, if she'd only try them, she'd feel instantly better. She never did; on the contrary she felt worse and worse. Perhaps the wilderness was the cause. Perhaps it was the forbidden fruit she had eaten. Perhaps it was a little of both, plus a touch of Eden-sickness. She had never known an hour's ill-health up to the moment when she had eaten the fruit and been turned out of the garden. The poor Man was distracted. He didn't care what he did or whom he robbed, if only he might hear her singing again and see her once more smiling.

What he did wasn't tactful; it only made the animals hate him—all except the dog and the robin—and brought new dangers about his head. It was the month of October and nights were getting shivery. He had scraped together fallen leaves to make a bed for her and had woven a covering of withered grasses. In spite of this, from the setting of the sun till long after its rising, all through the dark hours her teeth chattered. She cried continually; every time she cried, out in the jungle the hyena scoffed. The Man rarely got any rest until full day. All night he was rubbing her back, her feet and hands in an effort to make her warm. As a consequence he slept late and accomplished hardly any work. He didn't even have time to notice how all the animals were building houses. The Woman was so fretful that he never dared leave her for longer than an hour. The poor thing was forever complaining that God might have made her out of something better than a rib, if He was going to make her at all.

It was a colder night than usual, when the Woman was crying very bitterly and the hyena was doing more than his ordinary share of scoffing, that the idea occurred to the Man. The hyena was scoffing because he was comfortable; he was comfortable because of the heavy coat that he wore. The Man determined to teach him a lesson by taking his coat from him. It was another remedy; he hoped that if he clothed the Woman with it, she might grow strong. Telling her that he wouldn't be gone for long, he padded stealthily away, followed by the dog, and faded out of sight among the shadows.

They found the hyena in an open space which the elephant had been clearing the day before. He was seated on his hind legs, gazing up at the moon with his fine warm coat all bristly, scoffing and scoffing. He was far too busy with his ill-natured merriment to hear them coming. In a flash the dog had him by the throat, holding him while the man robbed him of his clothing. When they had stripped him of everything, even of his bushy tail, they let him go and he fled naked, howling the alarm through the forest. By the time they got back to the Woman all the underbrush was stirring. From every part of the wilderness, in twos and threes, the animals were coming together. The night was alive with their glowing eyes; the leaves trembled with their savage muttering.

"Be quick," whispered the Man. "Put this on."

She dried her tears as she felt the warmth of the fur. "It's comfy," she sobbed. "It fits exactly." And then, "Oh, Man, I'm frightened. What have you done? You gave me a present once before."

The Man was making a club out of a tree. As he stripped it of its branches, he answered boastfully, "It was I and the dog; we did it together. You were cold, so we stole the hyena's coat from him. All the animals are angry. They know that we shall do again what we have done once. They feel safe no longer. They say it must be stopped. They want to get back the hyena's coat from us."

"And they will, oh, my master," the dog interrupted, "unless we protect ourselves. Through the wilderness, not many miles from here, a limestone ridge rises above the forest. In the limestone ridge there is a cave. If we can win our way to it before our enemies come together, we can stand in the entrance and guard the Woman."

So the dog ran ahead growling with such fierceness that everything fled from his path. Behind him came the Man carrying the Woman very closely because he loved her, and trailing his tremendous club. By dawn, before their enemies could guess their purpose, they had gained the cave. By the time the animals had held their conference and decreed that the Man and the dog must be punished, they had escaped and were ready to defy all comers.

IV

From that moment a new and exciting kind of life started. Not an hour out of the twenty-four was free from anxiety. Always, whether it was day or night, the Man and the dog had to take turns at guarding the entrance. The Man gathered piles of stones and learnt how to throw them unerringly. The dog trusted to his teeth and the fear which his bark inspired. The animals were furiously determined; they never ceased from attempting to surprise them. Quite often they would have succeeded, had it not been for the robin, who hiding in the bushes, overheard their strategies and flew back to the Man in time with warnings.

The cave was well chosen. It was approached by a steep and narrow path. Only one enemy could attack at once, so the defenders were always able to roll down bowlders on him before he gained a footing. That was how they treated the lion, when he came thrashing his tail and roaring on the first morning to make them prisoners. They gave a rock a big shove and knocked him over like a ninepin. He was so hurt in his feelings that he sulked in bed for a week; for many more weeks he was easily tired. Seeing that he was the King of the Beasts and the President of their Conference, this made the animals the more indignant and the more determined that the Man and the dog must be punished. The next to attempt their capture were the elephant and the rhinoceros. They boasted that they weren't afraid of rocks; nevertheless they came together to back up each other's courage. Half way up the slope they stuck. They were too heavy for so steep a path. The ground crumbled from under them, the dog worried them, the Man struck them, and away they went, bumping down the hill, rolling over and over. They never stopped till they had reached the bottom, where they lay on their backs with their feet in the air, grunting and panting like a pair of upturned locomotives.

At first the Man and the dog regarded the enmity they had aroused in the light of a huge joke; they got a good deal of fun out of fighting. But the sporting side of the affair ceased to appeal to them when they were compelled to recognize the seriousness of their predicament. They were absolutely cut off from supplies at a season when food was running short.

They had to sneak out at night at the risk of capture to get anything to eat at all. They had a sick woman on their hands who cried not for food, but for delicacies. Instead of gathering strength, she grew steadily weaker. And then there was the matter of sleep; it was as scarce as food. They hardly snatched a wink of it. When they weren't on guard or fighting, they were soothing her fretfulness, foraging for her or thinking up some new method of keeping her warm. It was damp in the cave; sunlight rarely tiptoed farther than the entrance. It didn't take them long to discover that the hyena's coat had been as dearly purchased as the forbidden fruit that had lost them the garden. Peace, which they might have concluded in the early days, was now entirely out of the question. Even an offer to return the hyena's coat wouldn't have made any impression. They had carried hostilities too far; there wasn't an animal whom they had not wounded and who wasn't mad with them clean through from the point of his nose to the tip of his tail. Often and often, standing in the entrance to his cave, the Man would gaze longingly across the bronzy roof of the forest to the distant shining of the padlocked gates of Eden. He was farther than ever from the garden now with its tranquil blessedness. If only he hadn't learnt to steal! Stealing had been the cause of his downfall—first the forbidden fruit and then the hyena's coat. If he had been less enterprising and more obedient, he would still have been the friend of God. After a wakeful night he crept to the entrance to discover that the worst thing of all had happened.

"A worse thing!" you exclaim. "I thought you were going to tell us a cheerful Christmas story."

And so I am: but all the unfortunate part comes first—that's the way the robins tell it. If you'll be patient and read on, you'll find this is the very cheerfullest story that was ever told in earth or heaven. You may not have noticed that we've not yet come to the first laugh. The Woman has smiled and the hyena has scoffed; but no one has laughed. It's when we come to the first laugh that the happiness commences.

V

The worst thing of all that the Man discovered when he crept to the cave-entrance after a wakeful night, was this: with a terrible stealthy silence snow was drifting down so that even the distant shining of the gates of Eden was blotted out. It was frightening; snow had never fallen in the world before. If it had, the Man had not seen it. Within the walls of the garden summer had been perpetual. He stood there staring out forlornly at the misty sea of shifting whiteness. It chilled him to the bone. It seemed to him that the pillars of the sky had collapsed and the dust of the moon and stars was falling. Soon everything would be buried and the world itself would be no more. He looked at the calendar which he had scratched upon the wall. It was the twenty-fourth day of December. He wondered whether God knew what was happening and whether He had planned it. Then he gave up wondering, for behind him, from the blackness of the cave, the Woman called.

"Oh, Man," she cried, "I cannot bear this any longer!"

He groped his way to her and raised her in his arms so that her head lay on his breast. Even in the darkness he could see the glow of her hair, like the shadow of flame growing fainter and fainter.

"My Woman," he whispered, "what can I do for you?" And again he whispered, "What can I do for you?"

She pressed her face close to his before she answered, petting him the way she had been used to do in Eden. "Do for me? Nothing. You've tried with your remedies—you've tried so hard. Poor you! If we could only find God——"

"If we could," the Man said, "but——"

And then they both grew silent, for how could they find God when He had climbed back to Heaven, destroying the sky-blue stairs behind Him?

"Perhaps, He still walks in Eden." It was the Woman who had spoken. "If you were to go and watch through the bars of Eden till He comes and were to call to Him—if you were to tell Him that I cannot bear it any longer and that we're sorry, so sorry—that we did it in our ignorance— —" Without ending what she was saying, she fell to sobbing.

He didn't dare to tell her that the moon and stars were falling and that the gates of Eden were blotted out. From where she lay in the blackness of the cave she could see nothing; she was too weak even to crawl to the entrance. As he did his best to comfort her, "If we could only again find God— —" she kept whispering.

So at last, having ordered the dog to guard her, the Man departed on his hopeless errand. It was brave of him. He believed that in trying to find God, he would get so lost that he would never be able to retrace his footsteps. Before he went he kissed the Woman tenderly, begging forgiveness for all the misery he had caused her.

"But I caused it, too," she confessed. "It wasn't your rib that was to blame. It wasn't you at all. I wanted the fruit and we ate it together."

It was the first time she had acknowledged it; until then she had insisted that the fault was his solely. So in the moment of farewell she restored to him one little ray of the great, lost sun of flaming happiness.

VI

The air was so thick with falling snow that he was well-nigh stifled. His eyes were blinded as though they were padded with cottonwool. The flakes brushed against his cheeks like live things. At his sixth step from the entrance he had lost his direction. His feet commenced to slide; against his will he went avalanching and cavorting down the path.

At the bottom he lay panting for a time; then, because he was cold he picked himself up and went blundering on, not in the least knowing where he was going. Bushes clutched at his feet. Trees slashed across his face. He was inclined to weep, but checked himself, remembering that on one of those sunny afternoon walks God had told him that to cry wasn't manly. "And I must find God. I must find God," he kept repeating to himself. The only way he knew of finding God was by pressing forward. God had once confessed to him, "The reason I am God is because I show courage."

"Then I'll show courage, too," he thought.

Presently he found himself in the heart of the forest and began to breathe more freely. Avenues of giant trees stretched before him, which criss-crossed one another and faded into the gloom of twilit, colonnaded tunnels. He could almost feel the gnarled trunks bracing themselves and the crooked branches linking arms to bear up the weight of the down-poured roof of whiteness. As his eyes grew accustomed to the dimness, he saw the animals strewn flat among fallen leaves, their noses pressed between their paws, shivering with terror. Overhead birds and monkeys sat in rows, squeezed side by side for companionship, weeping silently. Of a sudden he regained his majesty, being filled with contempt for their cowardice. "For I am Man," he reminded himself, "so like to God that I could easily be mistaken for Him—and these are the creatures who dared to talk of punishing me."

Throwing out his chest, he strode valiantly past them, utterly ignoring their presence.

From behind him a voice called whimperingly. It was the lion's, the King of Beasts, squeaky and falsetto with panic. "Master, thou art wise. What has happened? Tell us."

Had he known how, the Man would have laughed. But the laugh comes later in the story. Without turning his head, still going away from them he answered. "It is a punishment for what thou and thy people have done to me and my Woman, oh, lion."

He had made the answer up on the spur of the moment; he knew no more than they did what had happened. But he loved inventing and was never so content as when he was pretending that he was God.

Immediately they forgot the wrong answers he had given them and how he had deceived them in the past. The leaves rustled as they lifted up their heads from between their paws. Their voices trembled as one when they besought him, "Master, stay with us. We are in terror. Make it leave off."

Turning slowly, he blinked at them through the dimness. Folding his arms, he regarded them thoughtfully with his legs wide apart. He did it as he supposed God might have done it. He spoke at last. "It's only just begun. Why should I make it leave off?"

"Because thou art strong and we are repentant."

Their manner was so humble and adoring that he felt sorry for them. They had begged his pardon in the same words that he had intended to beg God's. And then he was just—the only just creature that God had created. In his heart he knew that he had merited their revenge—there was scarcely one of them at whom he had not hurled his rocks. He came back walking in stately fashion till he stood fearlessly in the centre of them. Looking up through the burdened branches at the calamity which he did not understand, he commanded, "Leave off."

To his immense surprise, on the instant the snow ceased falling. It settled gently like a tired bird into its nest. The serenity of the stillness was unbroken.

"I am hungry," he said.

The animals hurried to their stores of food and waited on him.

"I have not slept."

The squirrels scraped fallen leaves into a bed, and the bear and the wolf stood guard.

When he awoke it was a brilliant winter's morning. The sun was charioteering in highest heaven. The forest was white as though cotton-wool had blown through it. As far as eye could search, everything glittered, sheathed in a film of glass. Snow bulged from branches like pillows filled to bursting. Icicles hung down like fantastic swords. Down the colonnaded avenues trees cast their shadows in heavy bars; the spaces between them were golden splashes.

The Man yawned. "I am still tired. Fetch the horse that he may carry me back to my dwelling."

He ordered the horse to be fetched because he had forgotten where his cave was. It was clever of him. He did it to keep the animals from knowing his ignorance.

The horse came galloping up obediently. Clutching him by the mane, the Man bestrode him. Off they started at a sharp trot, with the animals shouting and bounding beside them. As they travelled, the Man could hardly keep from smiling at picturing what a fine fellow he was. He made no attempt to restrain himself from giving orders. All the time he kept urging the animals to shout louder. He wanted the Woman to hear them, so that she might crawl to the entrance of the cave and be a witness of his triumphant home-coming. It wasn't good enough merely to picture himself as a fine fellow. He was anxious to hear her say to him, "Oh, Man, what a fine fellow you are!" He'd forgotten completely the purpose of his errand — that he'd set out through the world's first snowstorm in search of God.

So at last they burst forth from the forest and reached the foot of the slippery ascent. Because it was so slippery, the Man dismounted; the horse could carry him no further. Having commanded the animals to go on shouting for at least half-an-hour, he left them and commenced to climb the steep and narrow path. He had to go gingerly on his hands and knees.

There were places where he slipped back two steps for every one he advanced. By snatching at rocks and bushes, he dragged himself slowly to the turning which brought him in sight of the entrance. There, seated in the entrance to the cave, he saw ...

You must remember that by now it was the twenty-fifth of December. To remember that is most extraordinarily important. What he saw is so exciting that it deserves another chapter.

VII

He saw the Woman—but not the Woman as he had left her. She was no longer sick. She was completely restored. As in the old days her hair clothed her like a flame. Her face parted it into waves as though she were a swimmer. He could see the pink dimples in her knees where she sat and the marble whiteness of her feet, which flashed like jewels. She was again the darling who had delighted his heart when she had darted like a sunbeam across the shaven lawns of Eden; but now she was ten times more radiant.

What was it that had changed her? Her tenderness made a golden mist about her which inspired him with awe. He had had precisely this sense of sunny quietness when he had walked through those long, still afternoons with God.

She was unaware of him. Her eyes were deep pools of sapphire. She was smiling gently and brooding above something which nestled in her arms. He called to her softly; she paid him no attention. Far below the ridge, in obedience to his commands, the animals were still shouting. Was it because of them that she was smiling? Had the robin flown ahead of him to tell her what had happened? The robin was perched on her shoulder, fluttering his little wings and singing her his finest song. He called to the robin; like the Woman, the robin was too occupied to hear him. No, it wasn't because of him that she was smiling—he felt sure. Then why was it?

He gazed back on the dazzling landscape that spread away below him, hoping to find something there that would tell him. How transformed it was from the gloomy jungle that had been wont to threaten him! It was like a nest of down. From its farthest edge where Eden lay, a beam of glory spanned it with an orange path. It was this beam that made the golden mist about the Woman. To his amazement he saw that Eden's gates were open. Even while he watched they began to close, slowly and slowly, with the beam ever shortening, till at last they were utterly locked and barred.

The memory of lost happiness overwhelmed him. He turned again to the Woman. There she sat in the golden mantle of her hair, enthroned on the snow's pure whiteness. Creeping to her humbly, he fell to covering her feet with kisses, so great was his need of her.

"My Woman," he wept, "they are cold—so cold. Never again will I leave thee, not even to find God."

She bent towards him, lifting his chin in her hand. "I shall feel the cold no more. Put thy hand in my breast. Dost thou feel it? I have that next my heart which, though I grow old, shall keep me forever warm."

As he slipped his hand in her breast, she parted her hair and showed him. Kneeling beside her, he gazed down wonderingly at a thing that he had never seen before. He could find no name for it. It was like himself and it was like her also, only it was tiny and no thicker than his fore-arm. It had wee feet and hands, a rose-bud of a mouth and it was smooth and soft. Its head, which was the size of an apple, was covered with silky floss. Lowering his face, he sniffed it all over. It smelt sweet like the flowers that used to bloom in Eden.

"What is it?"

She shook her head. "It was here when I wakened." Her eyes became bright and immense as stars. "It's our's," she whispered tenderly.

VIII

It was awkward to have something for which you could find no name, especially when it was something that you had begun to love already.

"We'll have to ask someone," the Man said. "If I knew where He was, I might ask — — "

The Woman's face blanched. "Not God," she begged. "Because of the fruit we ate, He might take it from us."

Just then they were disturbed by a rustling of snow. Looking up, they saw the rabbit, watching them with timid eyes and recovering his breath after the long climb.

"What d'you want?" the Man asked sharply.

The rabbit flicked his white scut and sat up on his hind-legs, his whiskers quivering with excitement.

"I want to see it," he panted. "The dog's been boasting. I hurried because I wanted to be the first to see it. I'm so little; I couldn't do it any harm."

"Let him see it," said the Woman. "He's gentle. He might be able to tell us what to call it."

So the Man told the rabbit that he could have just one peep. But when the rabbit tried to get his peep by standing against the Woman's knees, he wasn't tall enough, so the Man had to lift him till he lay all furry against the little creature that was in the Woman's arms.

"I can't suggest anything," said the rabbit. "We ought to consult the other animals. They all want to be friends; they're so curious. But there's one thing I do know: we're both small and my coat would just fit it."

Before they could stop him, he had pulled off his coat and was tucking it snugly about the little stranger. He was right; it did fit exactly. So the first garment of the earth's first baby was a rabbitskin, which accounts for the rhyme which mothers sing about "Gone to fetch a rabbitskin, to wrap the baby bunting in."

When the rabbit had presented his gift, he hopped down from the Woman's lap very much thinner.

"And now can I bring the other animals?" he asked.

The Man hesitated. He was remembering the last visits of the lion and the elephant and the rhinoceros. "They might find a name for it," the rabbit pleaded.

Then the Man nodded and the rabbit scuttled off.

They hadn't long to wait before they heard a deep breathing and grunting. Struggling up the frozen path to the cave came all the animals that God had created. They advanced in single file, the great and the small mixed up together; the giraffe followed by the hedgehog and the mastodon preceded by the frog. They came hand-in-hand, forming a chain to pull one another up, treading on each other's heels, jostling and slipping back on one another. Those behind kept whispering to those in front to hurry; those in front were too winded to retort. Their ascent was made more difficult by their generosity, for all save one of them carried presents. The one who came empty-handed was the stork. He led the procession looking stately and pompous, as though he were taking the credit for having occasioned the disturbance. The Man learnt later that that was precisely what he was doing—taking all the credit. He had been telling the animals that it was he who had left the strange little creature at the Woman's side the night before. Because of this he pretended that it wasn't necessary for him to bring a present. There were many who believed him. There still are.

When they had all climbed safely to the top they gathered in a semi-circle about the Woman, having piled their gifts before her. In silence they waited; then she parted her hair and showed them the wonder that nestled in her arms.

The Man, standing at her side, addressed them. "Oh, brothers, I am wise, for I have walked with God; yet have I never seen anything like it. There was nothing like it in Eden. I have sent for you that I may ask you what to call it."

No one answered. He questioned each in turn, but none of them could advise him.

"We have to find a name for it," he said crossly; "so let's sit down and think hard."

So they sat down in the snow, scratching their heads, and thought hard. From time to time the Man enquired whether any of them had had an inspiration. They never had, which was discouraging when you consider what a lot of them were thinking. In this way at least an hour must have passed.

Things were getting both cold and embarrassing, when the little creature, who was being thought about so hard, showed signs of waking and began to stir in the Woman's arms. I ought to have told you that ever since the Man's home-coming it had been sleeping. First it kicked out with its bandy legs. Then it fisted its pudgy hands and yawned. Then it puckered its wee red face in a manner most alarming and, to the amazement of them all.... The Woman was so amazed that she nearly let it drop. And yet what it did was perfectly natural; it opened its eyes, like two blue patches of heaven, and blinked at them. Last of all it emitted a thin, wailing sound that made everybody abominably unhappy. The crocodile became so emotional that his tears froze in two long icicles. After a pause the sound was repeated. All the animals rose on their hind-legs and covered their ears with their paws.

The Woman stared at them apologetically. She was distressed and puzzled. "Please don't cover your ears," she begged. "And don't think that I'm hurting it. There's something that it's trying to tell us. It's said the same thing before. It began saying it the moment I first found it. It's gone on saying it, on and on.... There, there my little one, my belovedest."

As if to corroborate her assertion that it had gone on and on, it commenced to cry afresh. Out of politeness to the Woman, though the sound hurt them, the tenderhearted animals uncovered their ears and listened intently. This is what they heard, repeated over and over, "Baa-aa-by! Baa-aa-by! Baa-aa-by!"

They were all shaking with sobbing when the elephant, in his coarsest manner, lifted, up his trunk and snorted through it contemptuously.

"Stop snorting," the Man ordered impatiently. "There's no reason why you should snort."

"Isn't there?" The elephant shuffled to his feet to depart. Before he went, just to show his independence, again he snorted. Across his shoulder he remarked. "And you think yourself so wise! You want to know what to call it. Every time it speaks it tells you." It cried once more. "There you are!" The elephant trumpeted triumphantly as he seated himself at the top of the slide, having pulled his tail from under him preparatory to tobogganing down the path. "Don't you hear what it says? 'Baa-aa-by! Baa-aa-by!' It couldn't be put more plainly. It's asking you to call it baby."

As the elephant pushed off and vanished in a whirl of flying snow, the Woman turned to the Man with a smile of gladness. "The clumsy fellow's right. Weren't we the stupids? Fancy not understanding our own baby!"

IX

As you may imagine, all the beasts and birds went back to the jungle very discontented. They didn't see why they shouldn't have babies. They were wild to have babies. They talked of nothing else. No sooner had they got down the hill from visiting the cave than they turned round and started to climb back again. They kept urging the Woman to be frank with them and to confess how her baby had happened. Of course she couldn't confess, seeing that she didn't know herself. All that she knew was that she hadn't felt well since she had eaten the forbidden fruit in Eden and, now that the baby had been born, she felt completely restored. Such information wasn't of much use to the animals, for the forbidden fruit grew inside of Eden and the gates of Eden were locked. At last the Man had to interfere to prevent her from being bothered. He stuck up a notice at the entrance to the cave, December 25th. Mother And Child Both Doing Well. Don't knock. When the animals came to call, he prevented them from entering by explaining gravely that having a baby was a very touch-and-go business and left one decidedly exhausted. To have listened to him you might have supposed that he'd spent all his life in rocking cradles, whereas he was such a novice that, had it not been for the elephant, he wouldn't even have known that babies were called babies. Like all fathers he deceived himself that there was nothing he didn't know about baby-lore. What was very much more surprising, by whispering and looking secretive he managed to impress the animals with his new-found learning and paternal importance.

But what had happened to the robin while all these excitements were going on? The last time we mentioned him he was sitting perched on the Woman's shoulder, singing her his very finest song.

The robin, though you may not have heard it, has always been a most religious bird. He had made up his mind, the moment the Man had come back, that the first thing to be done was to go and tell God. The chief difficulty about accomplishing this errand was due to God Himself; as you will remember, in returning to Heaven God had destroyed the sky-blue stairs behind Him. But the robin had wings; moreover he was an optimist. He hoped that by fluttering up and up he would be able to reach Heaven in safety. The reason that he had never tried before was because he had been afraid that God would not want him. He felt sure of his welcome now that he was the bearer of such glad tidings.

He found the journey much harder than he had expected. There were parts of it that were so bitter that his wings would scarcely flutter. After he had lost sight of earth, he had to wind his way between the burning stars; they were so close together in places that his feathers were scorched. But he pressed on valiantly till he made out the quiet shining of the gates of Heaven and entered through the unguarded walls of jasper into a garden, which was in no way different from the one that God had planted upon earth.

Beneath scented trees the angels were scattered about disconsolately. There were black rims under their eyes; it was easy to see they had been worrying. Their beautiful white gowns had come unstarched; it was many days since they had tidied themselves. There wasn't a sound of any sort—least of all of music. Some of them still carried their harps; but most of them had stacked them in open spaces the way soldiers stack their rifles. When the robin sank spent to the grass in front of them, they paid him scant attention. When he weakly chirped his question, "Where's God?" they jerked their thumbs, indicating the direction, too listless to waste breath on words.

"What's the matter?" asked the robin.

"We're unhappy." After they had said it, they had difficulty to choke back their sobs.

"But why are you unhappy? Whoever heard of being unhappy in Heaven!"

"Because—because——." They glanced at one another forlornly, hoping that someone else would be the first to answer. "Because of the forbidden fruit. It's made God cross."

"Pshaw!" The robin swelled out his little breast with importance. "You'd better visit earth and see our baby. If the Woman hadn't eaten the forbidden fruit, there wouldn't be any baby."

The word "baby" was entirely new to them. They sat up beneath their scented trees and began to ask questions. But the robin didn't want to be delayed; he spread his wings and fluttered on.

At last he came to the smoothest of smooth lawns, in the midst of which grew a mulberry-tree, beneath whose shadow God was seated with the Virgin Mary. Despite the flakes of sunlight falling and the gold-blue peace by which They were surrounded. Their attitudes were no less despondent than the angels'. God sat with His elbows digging into His knees. His face was buried in His delicate hands. His eyes, peering through His fingers, were strained and red with always staring broodingly straight before Him. Of the Virgin Mary, crouching at His feet, the robin could only see the glint of her flaxen hair and the paleness of her narrow shoulders. Her head was bowed in the lap of her Maker as if she had been beseeching Him always.

The robin was overwhelmed with terror. All his chirpiness was gone. "Dear God," he quavered, "I beg Thy forgiveness. I have come when I was not bidden."

He paused, hoping that God would encourage him. When God took no notice, he felt himself to be the most insignificant and impertinent of living creatures. He spoke again, lest the silence should kill him on the spot.

"I have brought glad tidings—at least, we on earth think they are glad. The Woman, whom Thou didst cast out for eating the fruit that was forbidden, has been very sick. She has been sick since April till just before day-break this morning, when she miraculously recovered. At her side she found lying a little thing—such a little thing—so like to Thyself, oh, God. It has bandy legs and arms no thicker than Thy smallest finger. It has a baldy head, about the size of an apple, with threads of gold spread over it like floss. It has a pink, wee face and a rose-bud of a mouth. It's eyes are like patches of Thine own blue Heaven. And it's soft and cuddly. The Women calls it her 'Belovedest.' And it smells sweet like the flowers we used to breathe in Eden. We didn't know what it was. Even the Man didn't know. He summoned the animals to come and find a name for it. While they were sitting on their hind-legs, behold, it awoke and told us that its rightful name was baby. And now, oh, God, we birds and animals want to have babies. We're all trying to find out how it happened. And I want to find out most especially, because——"

"A baby, thou sayest! What is a baby? I, thy Creator, know nothing of it. The last thing I fashioned was the Woman, who has brought this deep shame upon Us."

God had spoken through His hands very softly, yet His voice was like a great wind blowing. It took the robin some seconds to recover from the shock. By the time he was ready to answer, the angels were rustling through all the glades of Heaven and the Virgin was gazing at him with wistful intensity.

"What is a baby!" he said audaciously repeating God's words. "It is a little Man and a little God. Surely, Thou knowest?"

"I know nothing," God thundered, letting fall His hands from before His face. "Be gone."

When the hurricane of sound had ended, the robin found himself hovering in the gateway between the jasper walls, where the sheer drop which lies between earth and Heaven commences. He turned to look back before he took the leap and saw that behind him the angels were following. Following most closely was the Virgin.

"Tell me again," she pleaded. "It's little and soft. It's cuddly and it smells like the flowers that bloom in Eden."

Perched on her shoulder, with his beak against her ear, he twittered to her his tale once more. While he was telling her, the angels crowded round, smoothing his feathers with shy caresses. But he didn't dare to stay too long, for distantly from beneath the mulberry tree, he still felt the brooding eyes of God. Launching himself from the Virgin's shoulder, he sank between the burning stars and through the bitter coldness of clouds snow-laden, till late in the wintry afternoon he reached the cave on the limestone ridge, whence a murmur of secret singing was emerging.

X

On the threshold he paused to listen. Yes, it was the Woman. It was the first time she had been happy enough to sing since she had been cast out of Eden. But her song was entirely different from anything that she had sung before. It was more little and tender. It was a lullaby of mother-nonsense, which she hummed when she couldn't find the proper rhymes and made up as she went along.

As the robin fluttered through the gloom to her shoulder, she pressed her finger to her lips to warn him. The baby eyes were the merest slits of blueness. The little thumb was in the mouth and the baby lips were sucking hard. The tiny knees were digging into the Woman's body and the baldy head was cushioned on her bosom. The dog snoozed across her feet. The Man crouched against her, shrouded in the mantle of her hair, overcome with weariness. She was mothering them all, rocking herself slowly and singing gently her silly little song. The crooning of it over and over seemed to hush them with a sense of security.

"You are my ownty,

Dear little donty,

Sweetest and wonty,

Pudding and pie;

Good little laddie,

Just like your daddie.

Fallen from Heaven,

Come from the sky."

"But he didn't," whispered the robin.

The Woman paused in her singing. "Didn't what?"

"He didn't fall from Heaven. God's just been telling me; He never heard about him."

The Woman smiled. "Never heard about him! It doesn't matter; his Mummy's heard about him." She stooped to kiss the soft little bundle, for he had commenced to stir. Then she resumed her singing.

Gradually the day failed. The late afternoon faded into evening. Gray twilight stole swiftly down. For a while the white fields of snow outside reflected a vague dimness; then night came with a noiseless rush, closing up the entrance to the cave with a wall of blackness.

Perched on the Woman's shoulder the robin dozed. She still went on singing. How long he had been dozing he had no means of telling. He was wakened by a multitudinous rustling, as of a crowd assembling and drawing nearer. At first he thought that it was some of the more persistent of the animals, coming once more to urge the Woman to tell them how babies happened. Then, of a sudden, he knew that he had been mistaken. The gloom of the cave was lit up by a glowing brightness. Peering across the threshold, with all the haloed hosts of Heaven tiptoeing behind her, was the Virgin Mary. It was the crowd of haloes that was causing so much brightness.

Stepping to the Woman's side, she gazed down longingly at the small God-Man.

"I want one. Oh, I want one so badly," she murmured.

The angels, thronging behind her, folded their wings and repeated her words, "So badly! So badly!" The sound was like a prayer, dying out in the void which spreads between earth and Heaven.

"Let me hold him," she begged.

Because she was the Virgin, even though it might wake him, the Woman did not dare to refuse her. But she asserted her authority, as all mothers must, by pretending that she was the only person who knew how to hold him properly. And perhaps she was the only one at that moment, for there was no other mother besides herself in earth or Heaven. She showed the Virgin how to support his little head because it was wobbly; and how to keep one arm beneath his back because it was weak; and how he liked to be cuddled against her breast because it was warm and cushiony. And then, becoming generous, she taught her the silly little lullaby.

"I shall never go back to Heaven," the Virgin whispered. "I shall stay here always and help you nurse him."

"Never go back to Heaven," the angels echoed; "stay here always."

The Woman's eyes became troubled. "But I want him to myself," she faltered. "I don't want helping." Then she ceased to frown, for she had discovered a stronger argument. "Besides, what about God? You wouldn't leave Him all by Himself in Heaven. He'd be lonely."

The Virgin nodded her head vigorously. "I would, for I also am a woman. There are no babies in Heaven. I couldn't be happy without a baby."

Behind her the angels nodded their haloes. "No babies in Heaven. Couldn't be happy without a baby."

It must have been so much talking that disturbed him; the baby woke up. As he opened his eyes and saw the Queen of Heaven bending over him, he smiled. It was his first smile. On the instant the Woman, like all mothers, became jealous and snatched him back into her own possession. She liked to believe that no one, not even the Man, could make him as comfortable as she could. Piling her golden hair upon her knees to make a pillow for him, she laid him naked on his back and commenced playing with his toes. If he had not given her his first smile, she would at least make certain of his second.

She was so taken up with her playing that she did not notice who had entered. She was the only one who had not noticed. The angels were cowering against the walls of the cave. The Man had roused and crouched covering his face with his hands. Only the Virgin stood upright, meek and fearless, with a look of unconquerable challenge. The Woman was quite oblivious; she went on with her mother-nonsense. And there stood God regarding her through a cloud of puzzlement and anger.

The game that she played with the baby-feet she was inventing on the spur of the moment. Starting with the tiniest toe, she wiggled it. Then she wiggled the next tiniest, and the next tiniest, and the next tiniest, till she had come to the biggest of the tiny toes. To each toe as she wiggled it, she gave a name; when she had wiggled them all she buried her face in the fat, kicking legs.

"And this is Peedy Peedy," she said as she wiggled the littlest toe. "And this next babiest is Polly Loody. And this in the middle is Lady Fissle. And this tall fellow is Lally Vassal.

And last we come of the big, big toe, who's king of them all. His name is Great Ormondon." Then she dived her lips into the little squirming legs and kissed them as if she were going to make a meal of them.

She had to do it four times before the baby smiled at her. At first he only looked serious and astonished.

The fifth time his smile broadened and he gurgled. But the sixth, as she came to "The Great Ormondon," he burst into a crowing laugh. Never before had a laugh been heard in earth or Heaven. It was so surprising that the angels ceased from cowering and the Man uncovered his face to see better.

Then God spoke. His voice was kind and tender like the cooing of doves — so kind and tender that the Woman, discovering His presence, wasn't a bit frightened. Sweeping the hair back from her eyes, she nodded to Him in the old friendly fashion in which she had been used to greet Him in Eden.

"Can you make him do it again?" God asked.

He came nearer and leant above her shoulder. So she made the baby laugh again.

"Could I make him?"

"Try," said the Woman.

So God wiggled the little toes, starting with the tiniest, and the Woman whispered the five magic names to Him secretly so that He might say them all correctly. "Peedy Peedy. Polly Loody. Lady Fissle. Lally Vassal. And the Great Ormondon."

When God boomed out the last large sounding name, the baby doubled his little fists, crowing and laughing unmistakably. Then God laughed, too, and the Virgin, and all the Hosts of Heaven, and the Man and the Woman, till at last the dog and the robin couldn't restrain themselves any longer and joined in His laughter. When once they'd started laughing it was difficult to stop. Besides, they didn't want to stop. They were doing it for the first time and they liked the feeling of it.

God laughed till the tears streamed down His face. By the time He held up His hand for silence, there was scarcely an angel who wasn't wearing his halo crooked.

"That's done us all good," said God. "I must have a baby for my very own exactly like him. I almost think that everybody ought to have babies." Then catching sight of the dog and the robin, He added, "I mean the animals, too."

He turned to the Man. "What day is this? I've not been counting since I ceased to walk in Eden."

The Man answered humbly. "Dear God, it is the twenty-fifth of December."

"I must remember that," said God thoughtfully. And then to the Virgin, "Come. It grows late. There is no one to light the lamps of Heaven. You shall have your desire; for you, too, are a woman."

And the robins say that God did remember, for it was on the twenty-fifth of December, centuries later, that his own son was born into the world. They say that the limestone ridge within sight of Eden was the spot where Bethlehem grew up after Eden vanished.

They even say that the cave to which Mary came on another winter's night, when the doors of the inn had been closed against her, was the very same.

There, where the world's first baby had been born, she wrapped God's son in swaddling clothes and laid him in a manger, for the cave had now become a stable. Perhaps the heavenly host who sang "Peace and Goodwill" to the shepherds was the same, though the robins do not assert that.

Of one thing they are certain: that every time a baby is born God laughs again and His laughter travels down the ages. And that is why on

Christmas Day everyone is especially kind to children, because it was a little child who gave the first laugh and taught grown people, even God Himself, how easy it is to love when one is merry.

THE END

Printed in the USA
CPSIA information can be obtained
at www.ICGtesting.com
LVHW071523301123
765241LV00085B/2716